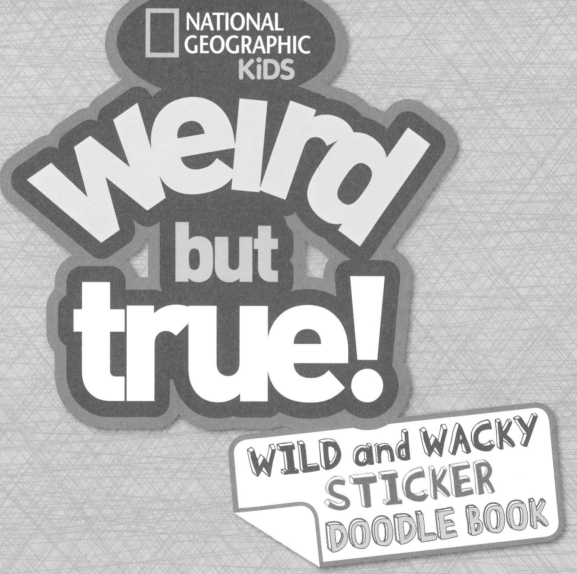

NATIONAL GEOGRAPHIC KiDS

weird but true!

WILD and WACKY STICKER DOODLE BOOK

NATIONAL GEOGRAPHIC KiDS

weird but true!

WILD and WACKY STICKER DOODLE BOOK

JOAN GOSSETT

NATIONAL GEOGRAPHIC
WASHINGTON, D.C.

COOL

WOW

WONDERFUL

ES YOUR TEMPERATURE, AND GIVES YOU MEDICINE. • BEAVER DAMS CAN LAST FOR HUNDRE
VE INVENTED A JACKET THAT CAN DRY ITSELF FROM THE INSIDE OUT IN JUST A FEW MINU
RLIER. • A 50-POUND (23-KG) OCTOPUS CAN SQUEEZE THROUGH A TWO-INCH (5-CM) HOLE. •
THE U.S. STATE OF MAINE. • AN ASTRONAUT ABOARD THE INTERNATIONAL SPACE STATION
D STOPPED TRAFFIC IN AUSTIN, U.S.A. • COCKROACHES LEAVE EACH OTHER MESSAGES THA
ENTISTS NAMED THE DINOSAUR SPECIES DRACOREX HOGWARTSIA AFTER THE FICTIONAL
ICKNAMED FOR A TYPE OF FRESHWATER ALGAE THAT CLUMPS ON ROCKS. MILITARY DOGS F
ANET. IF THEY'RE RUNNING OUT OF NAMES FOR THEM. • A STAR WARS FAN LEGALLY CHANGE
A BUILT MORE THAN 20 LIFE-SIZE MODELS OF PREHISTORIC ANIMALS IN HIS BACKYARD
LA'S GLASS SLIPPER WOULD LIKELY HAVE SHATTERED WHEN SHE RAN FROM THE BA
MPETITION IN ENGLAND. • SOME JELLYFISH GLOW. • LEMONS CAN POWER LIGHTBULBS. • MIL
IG AS THIS TOY CAR. ICE MELTS ON EARTH. • FIFTY-SIX MILLION YEARS AGO, H
NUAL REDHEAD DAY FESTIVAL IN THE NETHERLANDS. • A DOG NAMED YODA ONCE WON THE
AN CREATED KERMIT THE FROG OUT OF HIS MOM'S COAT AND TWO PING-PONG BALLS. •
RESTING. • A MONTH ON VENUS IS LONGER THAN A DECADE ON VENUS. • SOME SPIDERS S
TEN SKIN. THERE'S A BEACH IN THE BAHAMAS WHERE YOU CAN SWIM WITH WILD PIGS. •
TENTIAL MATES. • THE DWARF GECKO, ONE OF THE WORLD'S TINIEST LIZARDS, CAN FIT ON
RD "TYPEWRITER" CAN BE FOUND ON ONE ROW OF A KEYBOARD. • AN EXCITED GUINEA PIG
RGEST GARDEN GNOME IS TALLER THAN A GIRAFFE. • PEOPLE ONCE BELIEVED THAT THE BU
D, HE INVENTED HIS HANDS TO HELP HIM SWIM FASTER. • AN INVENTOR ONCE DE
RLD THAT IS ALWAYS BUILDING. A SCHOOLTEACHER OF THOMAS EDISON, INVENTOR OF THE
SHIONABLE ITALIANS WERE ONCE SO TALL THEY HAD TO WALK WITH SERVANTS TO KEEP T
O FEET (30 M) LONG. • IT TOOK 58 DAYS FOR A MAN TO WALK FROM PARIS, FRANCE, TO MO
AWK FLEW MORE CURSE WORDS THAT IT WAS REMOVED FROM HIS MASTER'S FUNERA
RK CITY FLEW AWAY AND HOPPED AFTER THE EVENT. FOUR TEENAGERS DISCOVERED 17,00
SCALY WAVES. THERE WERE MORE THAN 100 PUBLIC HOLIDAYS A YEAR IN ANCIENT ROME
NTS STRAIGHT. SOME BIRDS USE TOUCH-SCREEN COMPUTERS TO COMMUNICATE WI
LD IN A FLORIDA DISH, IT IS TOPPED WITH FROG LEGS, ALLIGATOR SAUSAGE, AND PY
ST POPULAR TOPPING IN THE COUNTRY. A CAT NAMED TUXEDO STAN RAN FOR MAYOR OF
OF ARIZONA IS THE SUNNIEST PLACE IN THE UNITED STATES. • AN ARIZONA LAW BANS F
S. HOT DOGS ENCASED IN FRENCH FRIES ARE A POPULAR STREET FOOD IN KOREA.
THE BALL IN TIMES SQUARE, NEW YORK CITY, WEIGHS ALMOST 12,000 POUNDS (5,44
ANNUAL LIGHT-UP PAPIER-MÂCHÉ PICKLE DROP FROM A FLAGPOLE. • TO CELEBRATE NEW Y
UTHERN AFRICA, PEOPLE CATCH, SQUISH, DRY, AND EAT GIANT CATERPILLARS CALLED MO
MPETITION, PEOPLE STAND ON TOP OF BARRELS AND THROW THE PUDDING UP TO 217 FEET
LED WITH MASHED POTATOES. • FREAKIES, QUISP, AND KABOOM WERE ALL BREAKFAST CER
OBE TWICE. • DOODLING CAN HELP YOU CONCENTRATE. • THE 16TH-CENTURY ITALIAN PAIN
STENING TO CLASSICAL MUSIC CAN HELP DOGS RELAX, A STUDY FOUND. • A DUTCH ARTIST
TH-CENTURY CHINA, PEOPLE WORE SUNGLASSES WITH LENSES MADE FROM QUARTZ, A TY
ERAGE PENCIL HAS ENOUGH GRAPHITE TO DRAW A LINE THAT'S 35 MILES (56.3 KM) LONG. •
MAURITIUS IN THE INDIAN OCEAN HAS COLORED SAND DUNES. • A ROCK IN JOSHUA
SEE A FUNGUS GROW IN THE SOIL. IT'S ONE OF THE WORLD'S FASTEST SNAKES—TH
-CREAM CONE. • MORE THAN 7,000 LANGUAGES ARE SPOKEN WORLDWIDE. • SMELLIN

4

of years. • A man in Oregon, U.S.A., lives in a retired Boeing 727 airplane. • reseal
• in 2015 someone found a message in a bottle that had been sent more than 100
archers discovered 1,500-year-old graffiti in Turke[y]. there are no poisonous
ed table tennis using a ball of water. • A 14-foot (4.3-m) inflatable pumpkin got
h microbes in their poop. • A building in Engla[nd]... it's windy outs
ol in th...

How to Use This Book

Welcome to the wonderful world of **Weird But True!** This fun-tastic series, brought to you by National Geographic Kids, features hundreds of awesome facts about **animals, nature, space, sports, culture,** history, and more, accompanied by amazing photographs. Inside this book, you're the master of this wonderfully weird world. You can bring the facts to life—or turn them on their head!—using your own smarts and creativity.

Grab a pencil or pen, and some crayons, markers, or colored pencils, and dive in! Soon you'll be penning a poem about swimming with pigs and exploring electrifying terms in a word search. Unleash your brainpower and imagination as you **doodle** and **draw, solve puzzles** and **quizzes,** color and connect the dots, **unscramble words,** and **fill in the blanks.**

Don't forget to use the 150 weird and wacky stickers to adorn your artwork and creations. Need help with answers? You'll find them at the end of the book.

Ready, set, turn the page and have a boredom-busting blast in

Weird But True!: Wild and Wacky Sticker Doodle Book.

Does he write his own songs? Help him finish this one.

One species of **bat** sings up to **100,000** songs in a **night.**

The moon shines above;
it's the nighttime I love ...
You turn my heart upside down!

Some eels have their **teeth cleaned** by "cleaner shrimp."

The shrimp even rocks back and forth to attract clients! Help it reel in customers by creating a sign.

DENTIST

An **artist** in Beijing made a **BRICK** out of the city's **dust pollution.**

Artists use discarded materials—including cardboard, cans, and plastic bags—to make all kinds of cool creations. What awesome artwork would you create with rad recyclables? **Draw it here.**

BONUS ACTIVITY!
With the permission of an adult, visit Recycle City
online at *www3.epa.gov/recyclecity* for lots of fun
activities. You can even take a turn as Dumptown's
city manager and clean up its littered streets!

In 2015 someone found a message in a bottle that had been sent more than 100 years earlier.

Do you have an important message or a secret to share? Write it down here.

Researchers discovered
1,500-YEAR-OLD
GRAFFITI
in Turkey.

Describe a typical—or extraordinary—day in your life through pictures on this wall. What will people think if they discover it 1,500 years from now?

Poodles are banned from participating in the Iditarod

This team of poodles is setting off on their own race across the U.S.A.! Where should they go?

12

There are no poisonous SNAKES in the U.S. state of Maine.

opossum

bear

That's a relief for Mainers, aka Mainiacs! The cool critters listed at the bottom of the page call Maine their home. Can you fit them all into the grid below?

crane

deer

turtle

fox

3-LETTER WORDS	6-LETTER WORDS	8-LETTER WORDS
bat	beaver	grosbeak
fox	fisher	squirrel
owl	marten	
	turtle	9-LETTER WORDS
4-LETTER WORDS	weasel	chickadee
bear		cormorant
deer	7-LETTER WORDS	
lynx	opossum	
	raccoon	
5-LETTER WORD	vulture	
crane	warbler	

grosbeak

A 50-pound (23-kg) octopus can squeeze through a two-inch (5-cm) hole.

It's a good thing they live under the sea! Find the 10 octopuses hiding in the nooks and crannies of this underwater scene.

An **astronaut** aboard the International Space Station played **table tennis** using a **ball of water.**

Now that's fun in zero gravity! Imagine how you would play your favorite sports or games while floating weightlessly. Draw and color your ideas here.

A man in Oregon, U.S.A., lives in a retired BOEING 727 AIRPLANE.

Are you on board with this cool idea? **Decorate the interior of your own airplane home.** Don't forget some reclining seats and tray tables.

Fingerprints can last for up to

40 years on paper.

Date:

Use some ink to make a fingerprint—or a handprint—here. Mark the page with today's date. Be sure to check back in 40 years to see if it's still here! In the meantime, create a drawing around your print.

A **14-FOOT** (4.3-m)
INFLATABLE PUMPKIN
GOT LOOSE AND STOPPED TRAFFIC in Arizona, U.S.A.

Help this pumpkin find its way back to the pumpkin patch before Halloween.

START

Pumpkin Patch **FINISH**

A **building** in England
SCREAMS
when it's **WINDY** outside.

The architect has apologized to the neighbors for this howling failure! Design your own noisy building. Does it burp or make other weird noises? Show us what your building has to say.

Military dogs **parachute out of planes** wearing tiny oxygen **masks.**

They're heroes! Design some medals for these courageous canines.

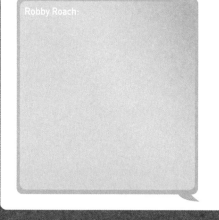

Rocky Roach:

Robby Roach:

Cockroaches leave each other **messages** through **microbes** in their **poop.**

Haven't they heard of texting?! What do you think they might say to each other?

Ewww! Don't slip on the rocks as you hunt for the funny names of other algae species in this word search. Words may be found horizontally, vertically, or diagonally, and forward or backward.

```
D O F G R E E P P I T Y Z Z U F Z Z Y T P
E S L R A E P A E S D E T A G N O L E I U
V O D E V I L T S U R C Y D N A G R U B G
I S D E E W E B O L Y R E H T A E L A F I
L T E N N E E R G U L F W E E D Z G O A W
S R E G N I F S N A M D A E D Z L U C E T
A O D R L E A F Y F L A T B L A D E A L T
P L A A J H P A I W T A L P R A E N E T A
R I E P E A C O C K S T A I L G R A P R L
O S D E E W E L B M U T A E S D E D R O F
N V F O N R E E R G M H Y D A E L Z Z U D
```

BURGUNDY CRUST
DEAD MAN'S FINGERS
DEVIL'S APRON
ELONGATED SEA PEARLS
FLAT TWIG

FORDED SEA TUMBLEWEEDS
FUZZY TIP
GREEN GRAPE
GREEN NET
GULF WEED

HAIR ALGA
LEAFY FLAT BLADE
LEATHERY LOBEWEEDS
PEACOCK'S TAIL

Imagine a new species of plant or animal that you might discover. **Draw it here.**

Scientists named the
dinosaur species
Dracorex
hogwartsia
after the fictional school
in the **Harry Potter books.**

Finish drawing this dino, then name it
after your favorite fictional character.

ARCHAEOPTERYX,
PREHISTORIC BIRD

SOUTH AMERICAN SHORT-FACED BEAR

Fifty-six million years ago, HORSES were the size of house cats.

JAEKELOPTERUS, GIANT SEA SCORPION

Millions of years ago there was a **bird** in Australia that **weighed as much as a POLAR BEAR.**

Someday you could do the same! Draw and color the backyard scene here, featuring some of history's most awesome ancient animals.

A man in Tennessee, U.S.A., built more than **20 LIFE-SIZE MODELS** of **prehistoric animals** in his backyard.

NAME CHANGE REQUEST FORM

CURRENT NAME

NEW NAME

REASON FOR NAME CHANGE

The *Star Wars* character YODA was originally named BUFFY.

On April Fools' Day 2016, the city of JUNEAU, ALASKA, U.S.A., temporarily changed its name to UNO after the card game.

A *Star Wars* FAN legally changed his name to DARTH VADER.

If you could change your name, what would you change it to? Fill out this Name Change Request Form, explaining which name you would like and why.

All of the letters in the word "typewriter" can be found on one row of a keyboard.

How many words can you make with the eight letters found in "typewriter"?

There are a lot! Write some of them here.

#1 pie	
#2	#21
#3	#22
#4	#23
#5	#24
#6	#25
#7	#26
#8	#27
#9	#28
#10	#29
#11	#30
#12	#31
#13	#32
#14	#33
#15	#34
#16	#35
#17	#36
#18	#37
#19	#38
#20	#39
	#40

The Dutch village of Giethoorn has no roads, only canals.

Row, row, row your boat! Plan your own watery village, adding whatever buildings and attractions you would like. Some suggestions are provided here:

- HOUSES
- LIBRARIES
- STORES
- SCHOOLS
- PARKS
- PLAYGROUNDS

Scientists have discovered so many planets they are running out of names for them.

Stars

Planets

Come up with some out-of-this-world suggestions for unnamed stars and planets.

U.S. president Thomas Jefferson was a paleontologist.

The bones of a giant ground sloth were even named after him: *Megalonyx jeffersonii*. Imagine if you found a fossil! What would it look like? Draw it here and name it.

Physicists think that
Cinderella's
GLASS SLIPPER
would likely have
SHATTERED
when she ran from the ball.

What do you think would have happened? Write a new ending to Cinderella's story!

Puppeteer
Jim Henson created
Kermit the Frog
out of his **mom's coat**
and two **Ping-Pong balls.**

A man once LICKED every cathedral in England.

CANTERBURY CATHEDRAL

You should never, ever lick a cathedral—or any building! But it's safe to get close to this word search, where you'll find art and architecture terms throughout. Words may be found horizontally, vertically, or diagonally, and forward or backward.

```
                          F
                      F   S   R
                  N   A   O   E   I
              M   B   C   B   A   V   E
          U   A   P   A   P   S   M   A   Z
          L   L   I   D   S   O       S   E   E
      O   C   L       E   D   M       S   I   L
  C   I   L       U   R   O               O   W   B
  O   A       C   E   E   N               E       B   A
  R   Y   I   E   E   I   F       O   V   E       Y
  N   A   R   A   R   C   H   P   T   O   W   E   R   E   N
  I       E   S   I   R   O   E       O   R   I       O
  C       N   O   P   R   R   R       D   A   P       C
  E       I   M   F   U   T   R       N   N   S       L
  Y       O   E   I   T   T   A   U   I   D   O       A
  O       J   Y   M       I   L   T   W   A   L       B
```

arch	cornice	joinery	spire
balcony	dome	mosaic	tower
bay	eaves	pier	turret
boss	facade	pillar	veranda
column	frieze	portal	window

SAINT PAUL'S CATHEDRAL

Washington, D.C.'s National Zoo offers art classes for its animals.

Help this golden lion tamarin finish its painting!

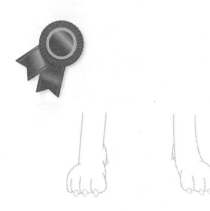

A dog named Yoda once won the World's Ugliest Dog contest.

Awww, he's kind of cute! Finish these drawings of the ugliest—or cutest—critters in the competition.

Some jellyfish glow.

What enlightening information! See if you can spot the electrifying terms hidden in this word search. Words may be found horizontally, vertically, or diagonally, and forward or backward.

```
        W O L R P
      Y E A F S D O
      Y R E T T A B S W
    E T U C O R T C E L E
  I G N I N T H G I L N H R
  F E L F E C H A R G E J O
  T E K R C H S O C K E T E
  D D C O S O E S U R Z H K
  P Y L D E H W S I G N A L
  I N E N V O L T A G E E
    Z A I M P C E M T
      L M F S U K P
        U O I R N
        L Y G R C
        O D N E U
        I E I N R R
        B L A T R
```

AMP
BATTERY
BIOLUMINESCENCE
CELL
CHARGE
CIRCUIT
CURRENT
DYNAMO
ELECTROCUTE
FIELD
LIGHTNING
POWER
SHOCK
SIGNAL
SOCKET
VOLTAGE
WATT

Lemons can power lightbulbs.

Crabs are distant relatives of spiders.

Here they are at the family reunion. What are they saying?

There's a beach in the Bahamas where you can swim with WILD PIGS.

Finish the poem!

This wild piggy went to swim class.
This wild piggy had a raft.
This wild piggy ...

There's an annual
Redhead
Day festival in the
Netherlands.

What color is your hair?
Finish these hairdos
and make them any
color you like. Don't
forget to add some cool hats
and other accessories!

Elephants can swim for up to six hours without resting.

Help this elephant find its way to the shore. Quick, time's almost up!

START

END

The world's largest
ROCK-PAPER-SCISSORS
TOURNAMENT
involved 2,950 participants.

What weird competition would you excel at? Draw it here.

There are approximately
three trillion
TREES
on Earth.

And thousands of species! Find the names of 16 of them in this word search. Words may be found horizontally, vertically, or diagonally, and forward or backward.

```
    E R D Y     Y
  M A G N O L I A     A
  I T U L I P O A K
R W I L L O W U W L D
O N G A M B H E O G S Y
E L P A M O E C N P O E
T U P E L O L R R I A D
A M L D C O U R S P
Y R O K C I H Y Y
    O E U S
  O E O U S
  W O S T
  D E L M
  R A D
```

ash
dogwood
elm
hickory

holly
locust
magnolia
maple

mulberry
oak
pine
redwood

spruce
tulip
tupelo
willow

42

WHEN THREATENED...

... a copperhead snake **releases musk** that smells like **cucumber.**

... the **hellbender salamander,** also called a **snot otter,** oozes clear **slime.**

If you could be a remarkable reptile, amazing amphibian, masterful mammal, or incredible insect, which would you be? Show or tell us about your best defensive move. Will it involve slime and snot?

An architect **built a bridge** out of **cardboard tubes.**

You have been asked to construct a bridge connecting these two islands. You can use any materials you want—even cardboard tubes! Draw your daring design here.

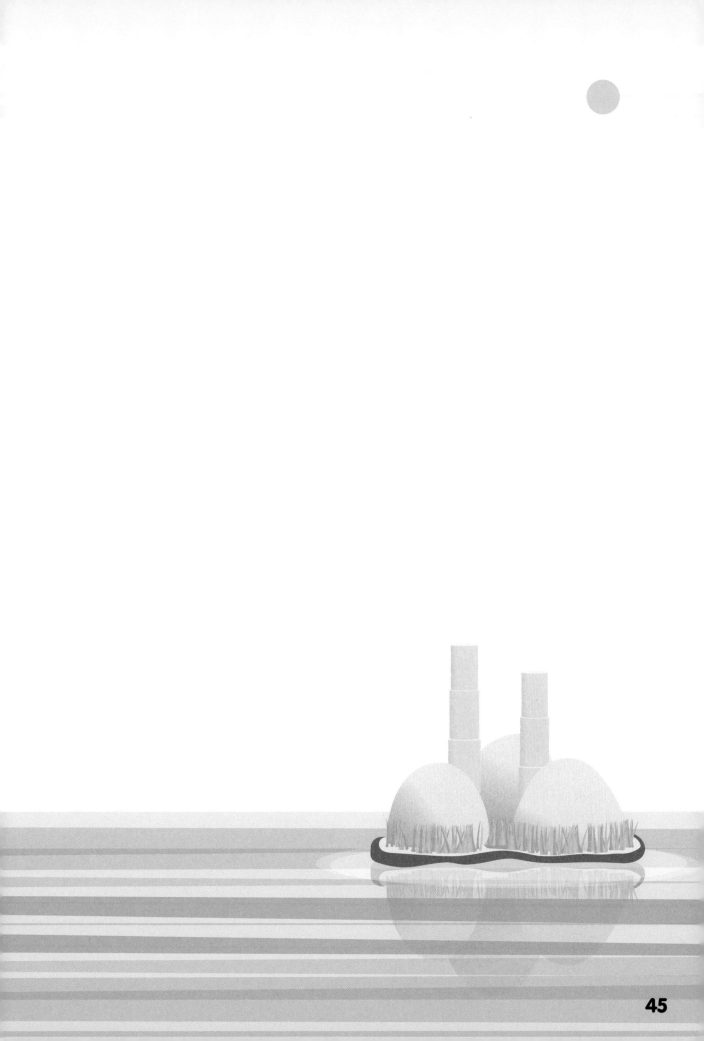

The first  STOP signs were black and white.

Can you convince people to STOP TEXTING when they're walking, driving, or biking? Design an attention-grabbing poster for your school or neighborhood.

TOADS do not have TEETH.

But they would look pretty funny if they did! Finish the drawing and add some toothy grins to these silly toads.

You're my mouse come true.
I like your big ears and whiskers, too.

This mice-tro has songwriter's block. Help him finish his song!

Male mice **sing** to attract potential mates.

A month on Venus is longer than a decade on Venus.

That's weird! Keep track of your schedule (or homework!) for the next month in this handy planner. You can decorate it, too.

Pink iguanas
live in the
Galápagos
Islands.

These rare and endangered iguanas need protection! Design a T-shirt that could be sold one day to raise money in support of conservation efforts in the Galápagos.

Galápagos

When **Ben Franklin** was 11 years old, he **invented fins** for his hands to help him **swim faster.**

Researchers have invented a **jacket** that can **dry itself** from the **inside out** in **just a few minutes.**

How inventive! You're a 21st-century scientist— *show us your creation.* Is it out of this world or down to Earth? Will it help you with your homework or help you live on Mars?

An inventor once designed **DIAPERS** for **BIRDS.**

Snail
SLiME
can be used to
soften skin.

Follow the trail of slime to the snail's hiding spot.

START

END

51

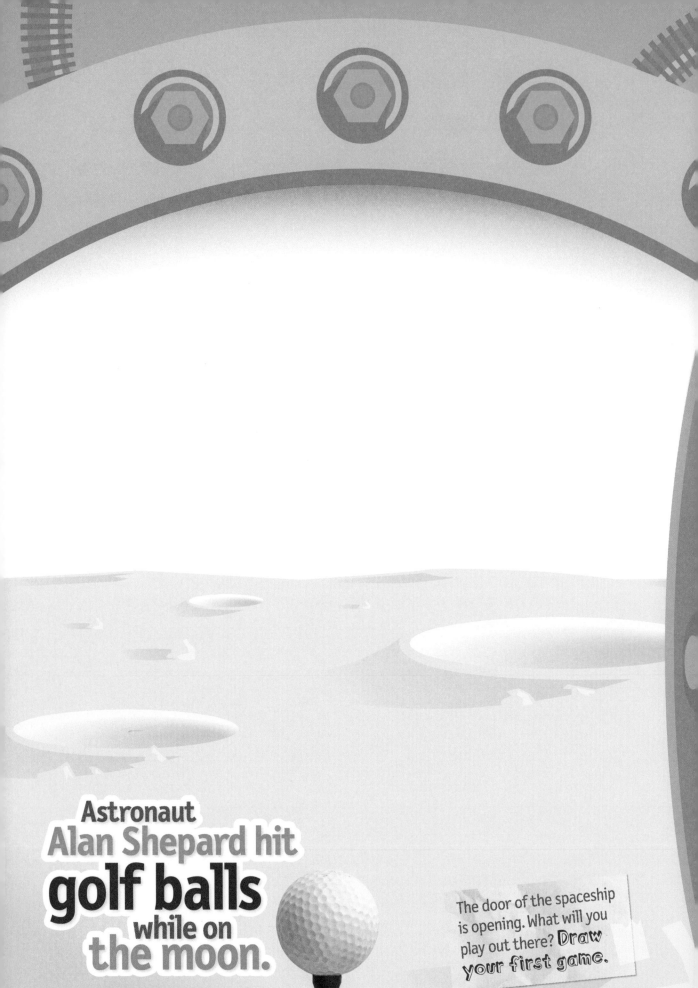

Astronaut Alan Shepard hit golf balls while on the moon.

The door of the spaceship is opening. What will you play out there? **Draw your first game.**

Some dinosaurs were the size of turkeys.

Gobble, gobble! Some even had feathers, but we don't know what color they were. What do you think? Color these velociraptors.

The **dwarf gecko,** one of the world's **tiniest lizards,** can fit on your **fingernail.**

What if you had a tiny pet that could go anywhere with you? What would it look like? Where would you go first?

People once believed that the **bumps** on **people's skulls** revealed their **true personalities.**

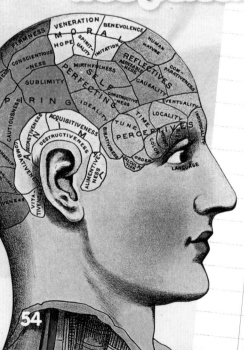

You don't have to analyze the bumps on your skull to know your personality. List the personality traits you like best in yourself and others!

Parrots talk without **vocal cords.**

What are these parrots saying to each other?

Find the 3 tiny garden gnomes in this yard—and 10 things that don't belong in a garden.

The world's **largest garden gnome** is **taller** than a **giraffe.**

WORLD FAMOUS GNOME
NANOOSE BAY ESSO

The scarlet ibis gets its color from the red crabs it eats.

What if it got tired of crabs and started eating scrambled eggs? Or limes? Or pizza? Draw what these ibises are eating—then imagine what colors they might turn.

An excited
GUINEA PIG
jumps STRAIGHT UP.

What do you think happened here? Help the radiant rodent record the good news in its journal.

Mount Everest
is getting
TALLER.

Quick! Color this picture of the mountain range before it gets any higher!

WINDMILLS OF SCHIEDAM, NETHERLANDS

BIG BEN, ENGLAND

EIFFEL TOWER, FRANCE

It took 58 days for a man to WALK from Paris, France, to Moscow, Russia— on STILTS!

Which cities or landmarks would you visit on a trip across Europe? Connect the lines from place to place to plot your itinerary. Be sure to draw yourself having an awesome time!

CATHERINE PALACE, RUSSIA

ST. BASIL'S CATHEDRAL, RUSSIA

BRANDENBURG GATE, GERMANY

BRAN (DRACULA'S) CASTLE, ROMANIA

COLOSSEUM, ITALY

ACROPOLIS, GREECE

A **schoolteacher** of
Thomas Edison,
inventor of the lightbulb,
thought he was too
"addle-brained"
to ever learn anything.

Edison had lots of ideas—
he held more than 1,000
U.S. patents! What are
some of your best
ideas? Draw them!

WEIRD

battery

The shoes of **FASHIONABLE ITALIANS** were **TALL** they had to **WALK WITH SERVANTS** to keep them from **FALLING OVER.**

Design some not-so-sensible (or sensible-but-fun) shoes for these fashion-conscious folks.

Some **ENGLISHMEN** once wore **POINTY SHOES** that stretched nearly **TWO FEET** (0.6 m) **LONG.**

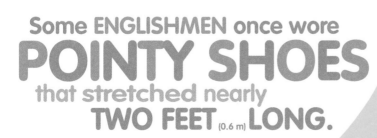

There was an **outbreak of contagious laughter** in an African town that lasted for **six months** straight.

Knock, knock.
Who's there?
_____.
_____ who?
_____
_____.

LOL! Make someone laugh with your own knock-knock joke.

A **cat** named **Tuxedo Stan** ran for **mayor** of Halifax, Nova Scotia, in Canada.

This cat is considering a run for president of the country of your choosing. *Support him or her with some campaign signs, buttons, and slogans.*

The first
giant helium balloon
used in the Macy's Thanksgiving
Day Parade in New York City
blew away and popped
after the event.

What kind of balloon would you like to see in the parade? Draw and color it here, then hold on tight!

Four teenagers discovered
17,000-YEAR-OLD
cave paintings by following
their dog into a hole leading into
France's Lascaux caves.

Draw and color these cave walls
to show future Earthlings what
life was like while you lived here.

100 public holidays a year
in ancient Rome.

Holidays

N	A	D	A	M	A	R	E	V	O	S	S	A	P	D
H	T	N	A	S	A	B	E	I	L	N	Y	E	P	I
A	D	A	S	O	P	A	L	T	W	O	A	T	W	E
S	C	H	R	I	S	T	M	A	S	K	H	M	A	R
D	A	E	D	E	H	T	F	O	Y	A	D	A	S	E
I	N	D	E	P	E	N	D	E	N	C	E	D	A	Y
O	B	O	N	R	M	Y	A	K	A	U	K	V	R	K
Y	A	D	G	A	L	F	S	V	W	N	Z	E	G	A
H	A	K	Y	U	R	G	I	N	D	A	H	N	I	O
L	O	D	O	P	I	K	A	L	J	I	N	T	D	B
P	A	L	S	V	A	D	G	M	A	Y	R	Z	R	A
Y	C	H	I	N	E	S	E	N	E	W	Y	E	A	R
H	A	N	U	K	K	A	H	L	O	V	I	U	M	A
I	G	O	N	E	W	Y	E	A	R	S	N	D	U	P

That's cause for celebration! Find the holidays and traditions of past and present hidden in this word search. Words may be found horizontally, vertically, or diagonally, and forward or backward.

Aboakyere
Advent
Basanth
Chinese New Year
Christmas
Day of the Dead
Diwali
Easter
Flag Day
Hanukkah
Holi
Independence Day
Kwanzaa

La Posada
Mardi Gras
May Day
New Years
Nyepi
O-Bon
Onam
Passover
Ramadan
Ridvan
Songkran
Thanksgiving

Now draw your favorite holiday memory.

Some
bonobos
use touch-screen
computers to
communicate
with **humans.**

These bonobos
are waiting to
hear from you!
Send them an email.

To: _____
CC: _____
Subject: _____
From: _____

Chimpanzees
can recognize one another
by their **faces** and their
distinctive-looking **rear ends.**

The "Everglades Pizza," sold in a Florida, U.S.A., town, is topped with **frog legs, alligator sausage, and python meat!**

Prepare these pies for your next pizza party with the wackiest toppings you can think of!

More than one-third of all pizzas in America are covered with pepperoni, the most popular topping in the country.

71

Cherpumple =
a cherry, a pumpkin, and
an apple pie stuffed inside
a three-layer cake

What weird food can you create? Make up your own strange recipe and draw the finished product here.

Olive oil and garlic are real **ice-cream flavors.**

During **World War II** people ate "**mock bananas**" made from **boiled turnips,** sugar, and **banana flavoring.**

Pets Deli in
Berlin, Germany,
serves gourmet meals
for **dogs** and **cats.**

These animals decided to open a place
of their own, and today's the grand
opening! **Help them finish
decorating.** Who do you think
will show up?

Listening to classical music can help DOGS RELAX, a study found.

This furry friend is chillin'. Put yourself in this easygoing scene with him.

HOT DOGS encased in **FRENCH FRIES** are a popular street food in South Korea.

School Lunch Menu

A Philadelphia, Pennsylvania, U.S.A., restaurant makes **TACO SHELLS** out of **BACON.**

These don't sound like healthy food choices! Help the school's cafeteria manager come up with a yummy but healthy menu.

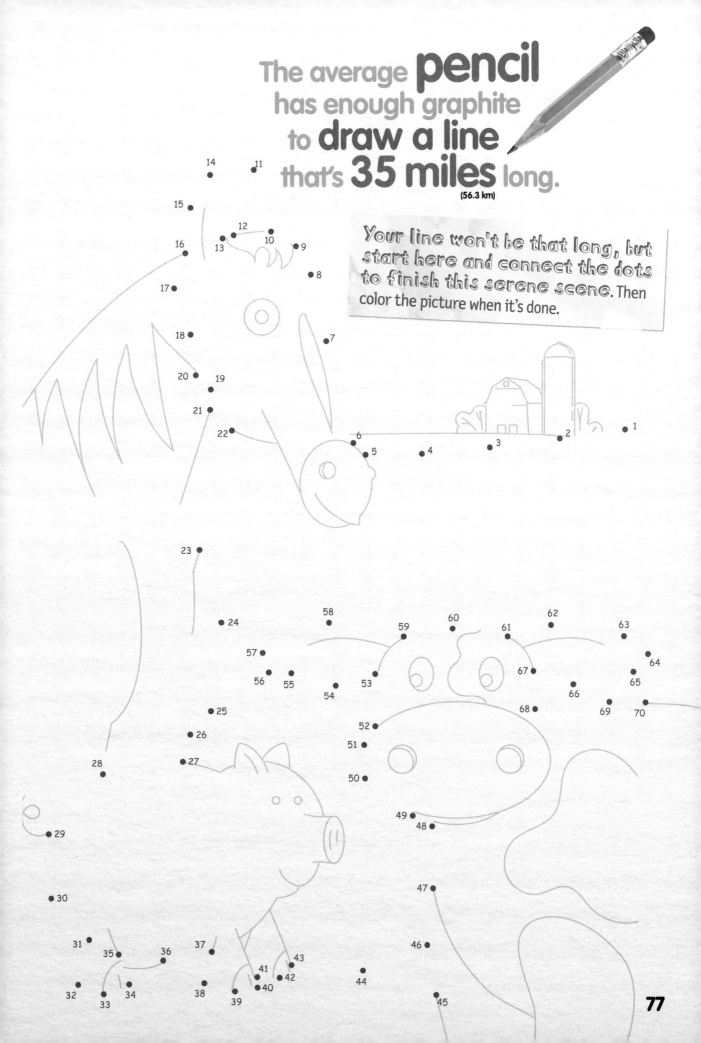

The average **pencil** has enough graphite to **draw a line** that's **35 miles** long.

(56.3 km)

Your line won't be that long, but start here and connect the dots to finish this serene scene. Then color the picture when it's done.

77

There's a beach in Hawaii, U.S.A., with green sand.

Build some *sand*-sensational structures of your own. Then invite some animal visitors. Draw them here.

You can visit
penguins
at **Foxy Beach**
near **Cape Town,**
South Africa.

A Dutch artist created a 69-foot-long (21-m) Wooden hippo

and floated it down London's River Thames.

This hippo wants to be on a swim team! **Add some other animals to his squad.**

This Peep is lost! Help it find its way back to the candy store.

START

PEEPS had WINGS when they were first made.

There are enough MARSHMALLOW PEEPS made every year to CIRCLE THE GLOBE TWICE.

END

candy-rama

81

Hippopotomonstrosesquippedaliophobia

The **face cards** in a deck used to represent **real royalty**— like Julius Caesar, Charlemagne, and Alexander the Great.

Who should appear on these face cards? Royalty? Celebrities? You and your friends? Draw and color the cards.

is the fear of long words.

That's a scary long word! How many other words can you make using its 36 letters? List them here.

Many **playing cards** in **medieval India** were **round.**

Africa's Nile River is longer than the width of the contiguous United States.

```
I R M M V P U R U S
A R I E D A M T N H
O T S K L V K O S A
Y C S O G I K A B T
A E I N A U N R E T
N V S G Y A I U P A
G K S I R T Y S H L
T O I A N Y G N N A
Z N P G A E E I O R
E R P L R L Y G Z A
V A I O A L N E A B
O N K V P O S R M N
R U M A C W I V A O
```

AMAZON
AMUR
CONGO
IRTYSH
MADEIRA
MEKONG
MISSISSIPPI
NIGER
NILE
OB
PARANÁ

PURUS
SHATT AL-ARAB
VOLGA
YANGTZE
YELLOW
YENISEY
YUKON

Dive into this word search and find the names of some of the longest rivers in the world. Words may be found horizontally, vertically, or diagonally, and forward or backward.

As a **training tool,** the **U.S. military** created a **plan** to **combat** zombies.

Yikes—zombies! Your country is counting on you to come up with a plan to stop them. **Draw or explain your strategy here.**

The
New Year's
Eve ball in
Times Square,
New York City,
weighs almost
12,000
pounds.
(5,443 kg)

10, 9, 8 ... ! What will drop at midnight at your celebration? **Show us your idea before December 31!**

To celebrate
New Year's Eve, people ...

... in Dillsburg,
Pennsylvania, U.S.A.,
watch a
three-foot-tall (1-m)
light-up papier-mâché
pickle
drop from a
flagpole.

... in Mobile,
Alabama, U.S.A.,
see the
12-foot (3.7-m)
mechanical
moon pie
drop.

It's impossible to see a full rainbow in the sky at noon.

Finish this rainbow before it disappears! Is there a pot of gold at the end ... or something else? Show us what's there!

One thousand years ago, **socks** were considered a **sign** of **nobility**.

Design some socks that are fit for a king or queen!

Smelling good scents, such as **roses**, when you sleep may give you **happy dreams.**

Sweet dreams! Have you had any happy, funny, or just plain weird dreams lately? Draw one here.

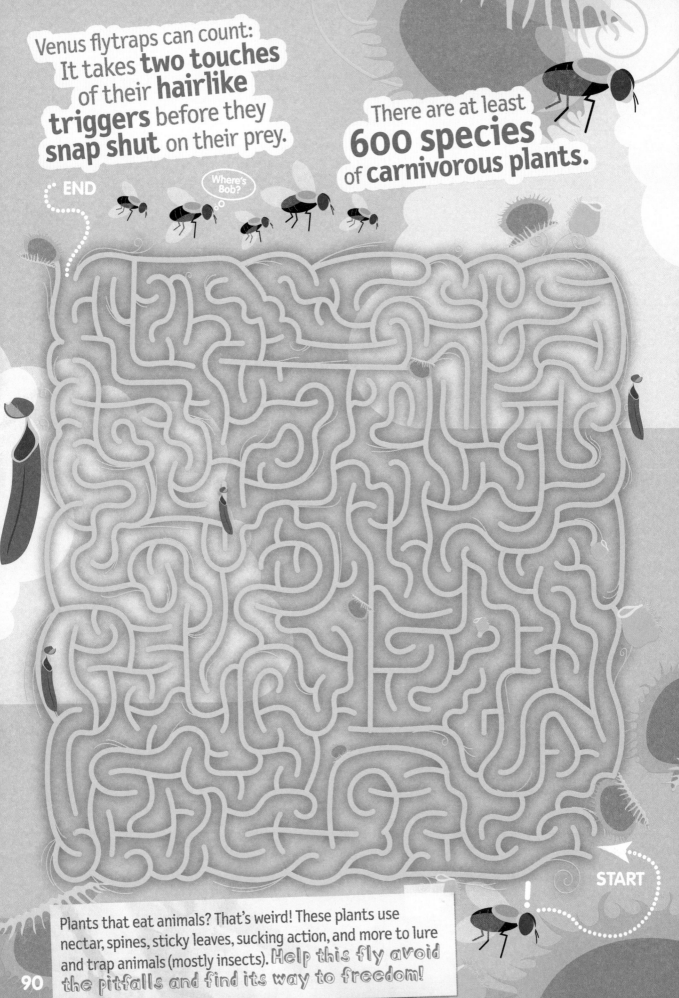

Venus flytraps can count: It takes **two touches** of their **hairlike triggers** before they **snap shut** on their prey.

There are at least **600 species** of **carnivorous plants.**

END

Where's Bob?

START

Plants that eat animals? That's weird! These plants use nectar, spines, sticky leaves, sucking action, and more to lure and trap animals (mostly insects). **Help this fly avoid the pitfalls and find its way to freedom!**

Find the seven differences between these two photographs of a tennis match.

Hint: The tennis balls are yellow!

Tennis balls used to be **black or white.** They were **changed to yellow** when it was discovered that **TV viewers** could **see them better.**

One of the world's
fastest snakes—
the **BLACK MAMBA—**
slithers up to
seven miles an hour.
(11 km/h)

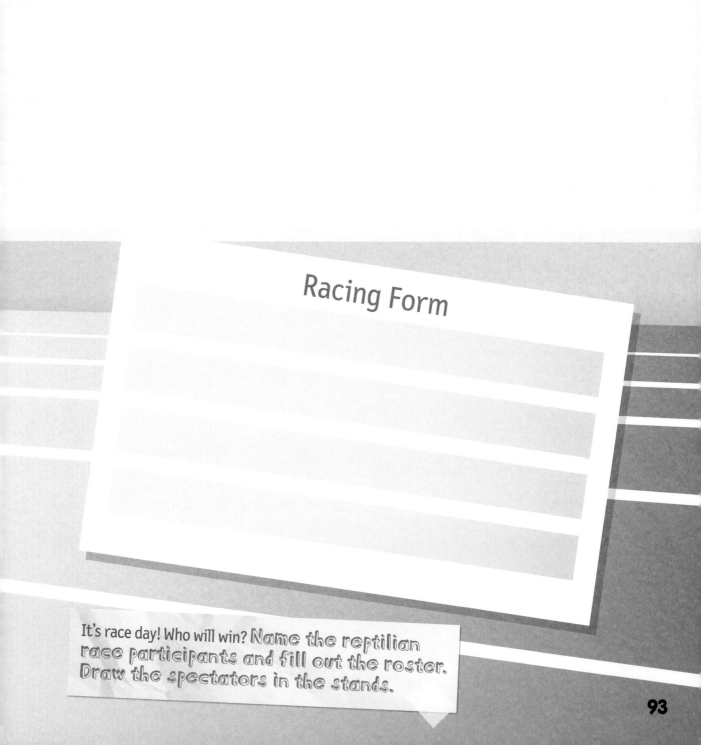

Racing Form

It's race day! Who will win? Name the reptilian race participants and fill out the roster. Draw the spectators in the stands.

Inky the octopus **escaped** from his tank in a New Zealand aquarium, **scooted** across the floor, and **slid** down a pipe that drains into the ocean.

What a supersmart cephalopod! Draw and color an undersea scene imagining what Inky's new life is like.

Some bacteria eat electricity.

Scientists are placing batteries into gold mines to lure the organisms from their deep underground world. Show what might happen when creatures come out—hungry for electricity!

battery

In the town of Marfa, Texas, U.S.A., mysterious twinkling colored lights appear randomly in the sky.

```
                        N
            E           E           E
            C   I       M       S   B
        T   H   O       K   Y   A       U
        J   O   G       M   S   R   N       L
        N   M   E   T   E   E   O   R   Y   A
        N   T   S   E   P   I   T   A   T
    P   A   U   R   P   T   I   W   E   F
    E   O   I   O   I   A   B   Y   N   S
    U   P   R   I   D   L   L   K   A   P
    M   I   D   G   L   A   L   L
    Y   S   S   I   E   C   I   P
        U   B   T   K   M   O   Y
        B   K   S   H   A   X   Y
    V   H   N   O   G   E   R
T   D   O   L       A
F   C   E
R
```

Peer into the telescope and find these 12 objects in the sky. Words may be found horizontally, vertically, or diagonally, and forward or backward.

asteroid	Milky Way	comet	Sirius
meteor	black hole	nebula	exoplanet
Big Dipper	moon	constellation	star

MARFA'S MYSTERY LIGHTS
VIEWING AREA
1 MILE

As part of a beaver relocation effort, **76 beavers parachuted** into the Idaho, U.S.A., wilderness.

If only the beavers could have kept a diary of their pioneering adventure! *Turn this beaver's diary entry on its head by asking your friends or family to fill in the blanks!* Then read the story back to them for a laugh.

Today we continued building the _____

Using lots of _____, _____ . My dad can fell tall trees with his own _____!
(NOUN)   (NOUN, PLURAL)   (NOUN, PLURAL)

_____, and _____
(NOUN, PLURAL)

_____ . Farther down the way, another _____ , we made it very
(ADJECTIVE)   (NOUN, PLURAL)

along the riverbank. A(n) _____ _____ family is _____ a den
                          (KIND OF ANIMAL)   (VERB ENDING IN -ING)

_____ . It's very cool. Earlier, my mom nursed my baby sister, called a(n) _____
(NOUN)   (ADJECTIVE)   (NOUN)   is also under construction in the middle of a(n)

She was born in _____ , along with my _____ other siblings. I turned two this year, and I'm excited to go off on
                (TIME OF THE YEAR)   (NUMBER)   (NOUN)

my own soon. Now I'm going to get something to eat. I'm in the mood for some _____ and

_____ .
(KIND OF FOOD)   (KIND OF FOOD)

Beaver dams can last for **hundreds** of years.

A beaver's **home** is called a **lodge.**

98

SEA STARS push their STOMACHS out through their MOUTHS and DIGEST FOOD OUTSIDE their bodies.

Which animals—other than a sea star!—would you invite over to your house? Draw your guests and yourself at the table, then fill in the rest of the scene to show us where you are and what's for dinner.

Bonus activity!
Grab a parent or other adult and go online to find out what sea stars like to eat at kids.nationalgeographic.com/animals/sea-star.

It is tradition to hide a **small plastic baby** inside a King Cake, a purple, green, and gold dessert eaten during **Mardi Gras.**

Tell us about the holiday or tradition you most look forward to and why. Then draw a picture of your favorite holiday foods, decorations, or costumes!

Chinese **New Year** is celebrated for **15 days.**

When **George Washington** was inaugurated as the **first president** of the United States, in 1789, he had only **one real tooth left.**

Washington's dentist crafted him dentures out of hippopotamus ivory and real human teeth! *Add teeth to these superlative smiles.*

The earliest version of the **penny** said **"Mind Your Business,"** not **"In God We Trust."**

That seems too weird to be true. (But it is!) If you could design your own paper money or coin, what would it look like? **Draw and color it here.**

A Tokyo company takes clients' **STUFFED ANIMALS ON TRIPS** and **SENDS POSTCARDS** to the owners.

TICKET

Destination:

Gate:

Where is your stuffed animal off to? **Choose a destination, draw your pal, and be sure they make the flight!**

x

5,000 = number of types of bacteria living in just .002 pound of soil (1 g)

1,400,000 = number of earthworms in one acre of crops (0.4 ha)

Hooray for dirt, worms, puddles, mud pies—and growing things! What will you plant next spring, or when you have your own plot? Plan your garden—or a whole farm—here.

103

A Canadian
company makes
PANTS
for DOGS.

It's Fashion Week for pets! Design an outfit
for your favorite animal friend.

The rocks in the Grand Canyon are older than the oldest known dinosaurs.

Be a rock star! **See if you can unearth 13 different kinds of rocks in this word search.** Words may be found horizontally, vertically, or diagonally, and forward or backward.

chalk
flint
granite
igneous
limestone
marble
metamorphic
obsidian
pumice
sandstone
sedimentary
shale
slate

```
                  F
    K G   E H E L L
    L R L G R A N I E
    A A E L B R A M N
    C H N A I D I S B O T
    S C I H P R O M A T E M
    Y R A T N E M I D E S S F
      I E C I M U P I D U L
      L I M E S T O N E
      S L A T E B G A
      I G N E O U S
```

An endurance athlete set sail off the coast of Florida, U.S.A., in a **GIANT INFLATABLE BUBBLE.**

Draw a picture of the most heart-stopping oceangoing vessel you can think of.

VIKING SHIPS sailed at about the speed you ride your **BIKE.**

A **SPERM WHALE** can dive
deeper than humans in the **deepest** diving
SUBMARINE.

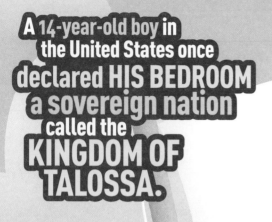

A **14-year-old boy** in **the United States** once **declared HIS BEDROOM a sovereign nation** called the **KINGDOM OF TALOSSA.**

What would you name your new nation?
Design your flag, then list the first three things you would accomplish as your country's leader.

1.

2.

3.

Every zebra's **STRIPE PATTERN** is **DIFFERENT.**

These zebras have been stripped of their stripes!
Create some patterns for them.

A zebra's **SKIN IS BLACK;** only its **FUR IS STRIPED.**

Ants as big as a **toy car** once marched on **Earth.**

Ant colonies can build **subterranean nests** that stretch **12** feet (4 m) down into the ground.

What are they doing down there?! Draw the ants in their colony.

Some dinosaurs lived in the Arctic.

Brrr! Draw your favorite dino and design him a cozy outfit so he doesn't get cold.

You won't believe what happened when my friend _____ and I visited Nature
(FRIEND'S NAME)

Adventure Game Land. We slipped on some virtual reality (VR) headsets and _____
(PAST-TENSE VERB)

into an undersea zone. Fish and _____ were everywhere. A pufferfish _____
(NOUN, PLURAL)   (PAST-TENSE VERB)

around our heads. A crab _____ my toe. Then a sea cucumber, feeling threatened,
(PAST-TENSE VERB)

ejected its organs in defense! "Ew, that's _____!" I yelled. We _____ and
(ADJECTIVE)   (PAST-TENSE VERB)

were face-to-face with a hagfish. Within seconds, we were covered in _____.
(SOMETHING WET AND STICKY)

"_____!" _____ yelled. "This way!" I called, heading down a hall. Soon it
(SILLY WORD)   (SAME FRIEND'S NAME)

was warmer, and our _____ sunk into hot _____. A small reptile stood
(BODY PART, PLURAL)   (NOUN)

next to a(n) _____ _____ mound. A Texas horned lizard! We started to
(ADJECTIVE)   (NAME OF INSECT)

_____, but it was already _____. Blood shot from its eyelids, hitting us!
(VERB)   (A FEELING)

_____ _____ through a door, we saw a sign: "Mediterranean Habitat."
(VERB ENDING IN -ING) (ADVERB)

A(n) _____ drank from a(n) _____ lake. The scene was peaceful and
(NOUN)   (ADJECTIVE)

_____. Then a newt ran to hide behind a(n) _____. Startled, _____
(ADJECTIVE)   (NOUN)   (SAME FRIEND'S NAME)

kicked some _____ _____ into the water. The newt's chest puffed. Spiny
(ADJECTIVE)   (NOUN, PLURAL)

ribs punctured its skin, oozing a toxin. "_____!" I yelled. "An Iberian ribbed newt!"
(EXCLAMATION)

We yanked off the headsets. "These animals need their space!" I called to the attendant as we

ran out the door.

Clever moths! Learn about some other awesome defense mechanisms by completing this short story. Ask a friend to fill in the blanks, then read the story aloud!

Some MOTHS emit
ULTRASONIC
CLICKS to jam
BATS' RADAR.

In Denmark there is a **model** of the **Statue of Liberty** made of **LEGO** bricks.

Great Sphinx of Giza, Egypt

Grab a pencil and finish building these monumental monuments. Add your own finishing touches to them, if you like!

Egypt's **Great Pyramid of Giza** is the only ancient wonder of the world that is **still standing.**

Taj Mahal, India

Your FINGERNAILS take SIX MONTHS to GROW from BASE to TIP.

A MAN in India GREW the NAILS on HIS LEFT HAND to nearly 30 FEET LONG!
(9 m)

What's the wildest, wackiest look you can give these nails?

In 1844 the Philippines officially skipped January 31.

If you could skip one day of the year, which would it be and why?

A mall
in the desert city
of Dubai, United Arab Emirates,
makes snow
for an indoor
ski resort.

Design a winter wonderland in this immense enclosed structure, where there will be plenty of fresh snow year-round.

EXIT

At a gym in British Columbia, Canada, you can take a yoga class while bunnies hop around the room.

What a hopping good time! Show us what it might look like if bunnies totally took over this gym.

All of today's pet hamsters can be traced back to one hamster family that lived in Syria in 1930.

This hamster family tree has some missing links. Fill in the missing family members and name them all!

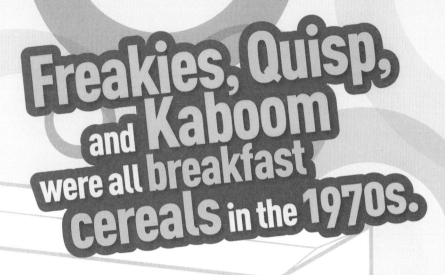

Freakies, Quisp, and Kaboom were all breakfast cereals in the 1970s.

You're the proud owner of a new cereal company! What does your cereal look like? What's in it? Design the box and come up with a good name.

You're not supposed to play with your food! But you can unscramble the names of the ones listed here.

In a **Scottish Haggis-Hurling Competition,** people **stand on top of barrels** and **throw** the **pudding** up to **217 feet.**
66.1 m

At a **summer festival in Barnesville, Minnesota,** U.S.A., **wrestlers compete** in a **ring filled** with **mashed potatoes.**

IBCORLOC

AANNBA

HPTESGITA

TETLECU

OCABN

CZUHICNI

AEP

OATTOP

NCHEKIC

DARBE

YTUGOR

EIC RCAME

PEPLA

HIFS

CEIR

Scientists have figured out a way to make **spider silk** using **goats' milk.**

These hardworking goats have been chosen to model clothes sewn from superstrong fabric made with spider silk. *What will they wear? Sketch out your ideas here.*

Some people hire **goats** to **mow** their **lawns.**

Every 13 or 17 years, **millions of noisy cicadas** emerge from **underground.**

A male African cicada can make a **sound** as **loud** as a **power mower.**

END

These cicadas need to tunnel out to make it aboveground! *Help them find their way to the top.*

START

121

During **World War II** kids were offered **carrots** on a **stick** instead of **ice cream.**

You don't see those on a menu very often! Fill these plates with some mix-and-match food creations of your own.

A cornflake shaped like the state of Illinois, U.S.A., sold for $1,350.

These flakes look like crispy U.S. states! Identify as many of them as you can.

The Sunshine State:

The Empire State:

The Pine Tree State:

The Gem State:

The Golden State:

The Pelican State:

The Sooner State:

The Lone Star State:

The Great Lakes State:

The Old Dominion:

123

Dalmatians are born without spots.

Awww, these brand-new puppies need some spots and tails to wag! Finish the drawings. Don't forget to name them!

Stonewise, Sturdy, and Hardy were popular names for dogs in medieval times.

A newborn puppy can take up to two months to start wagging its tail.

124

An
eagle can
spot a **rabbit**
from more than
a **mile away.**
(1.6 km)

Clever predators! Draw some predators in action below. Who do they have their eye on? Draw their prey, too!

A small Amazon
rain forest spider
weaves **decoys**
of **bigger spiders**
into its webs to keep
predators away.

Male woodchucks are called HE-CHUCKS; females are called SHE-CHUCKS.

That sentence is *almost* a tongue twister. Fill in the blanks below to make some fun and tough tongue twisters. Use the suggested words or think up your own.

Nouns starting with ch

cheese
chicken
chili
chickadees

A he-chuck chews chunky _____.
(noun starting with ch-)

The she-chuck should_____ a _____.
(verb starting with s-)   (noun starting with sh-)

_____

_____

_____

_____

_____

_____

Verbs starting with s

see
sway
sell
surprise

Nouns starting with sh

sheep
sheepdog
shadow
shamrock

Scientists found bits of a date stuck in the teeth of **a 40,000-year-old Neanderthal.**

Someone forgot to floss! Design a poster for your bathroom so you won't forget to brush and floss. Come up with a sparkling slogan.

You might need a toothpick to get rid of **toothpack,** the food that gets **stuck in your molars.**

U.S. president Thomas Jefferson served macaroni and cheese at a state dinner.

Appetizer

Soup

Vegetable

Entree

Dessert

That sounds unusual—and awesome! If you were going to visit the White House, which of your favorite foods would you want to see on the menu?

After all three of his wins at Wimbledon, a Serbian tennis pro celebrated by eating grass off the court.

My Accomplishment

Favorite Way to Celebrate

Person I Shared the News With

Next time he should bring some salad dressing! What are your favorite ways to celebrate a win in school, at home, or on the playing field? Tell us all about your best or most fun accomplishment.

A sheep, a duck, and a rooster were the first passengers on a hot air balloon.

Up, up, and away! Draw yourself and three guests inside the basket of this bodacious balloon.

Yuma, Arizona, is the sunniest place in the United States.

There's rain today in Yuma.
No one is sneezing—
So quiet when it's cloudy.

There's rain to day in Yuma.
No one is sneezing—
So quiet when it's cloudy.

These sunny facts inspired a haiku—a poem that has seven syllables in the first and last lines and five syllables in the middle line. Write one yourself. (It doesn't have to be about Yuma!)

One in three people sneeze after looking at the sun.

A CAFÉ in JAPAN offers SOLO CUSTOMERS a GIANT STUFFED ANIMAL to KEEP them COMPANY while they eat.

Who's sitting across from you at the café? Which stuffed animal would you bring with you?

moomin House

An Englishman once pedaled around the world on a big-wheeled bicycle called a penny-farthing.

Wheeee—bikes have come a long way! **Finish these drawings and then draw your own bike or one you would like to ride.**

Some of the earliest bicycles had no pedals.

Connect the dots.

A **five-seat bicycle** is called a **quindem.**

Gelotology is the study of LAUGHTER.

Be a good student and write your own joke!

Knock, knock.

Who's there?

Orange.

Orange who?

Orange you going to write your own knock-knock joke?

Knock, knock.

Who's there?

_____

_____

_____

_____

_____

Knock, Knock.

Windmills have been used for more than 4,000 years.

Energy shortages and pollution? The answer—or one of them—is blowing in the wind! Design a windmill for your town or your own backyard.

A **herd** of **COWS** wandered onto the cyclists' route during the 2015 Tour de France.

Mooove out of the way! Help these cyclists find their way around the obstacles to the finish line.

START

FINISH

A dairy cow produces about **100,000** glasses of milk in its lifetime.

A camel can drink **500** cups of water (118 L) in **10** minutes.

Gulp! **Fill these bottles with your favorite beverages**—or make up your own—then create some cool labels for them.

It took an ultra-marathoner 46 days, 8 hours, and 7 minutes to hike the 2,189 miles (3,523 km) of the Appalachian Trail.

What a trailblazer! Unscramble the names of all the states that this famous footpath passes through.

TCNIECCNUTO

GGOIEAR

ASACTSHUMESTS

RNMYLADA

IMNAE

TORNH AIROCLAN

WNE ARHMSIPEH

ENW YEREJS

NIENSPVALNAY

ESTNEESEN

IIRNIVAG

NMEVROT

ETWS INRIVIAG

Herring release bursts of bubbles from their rear ends to communicate.

What do you think these water-dwelling animals are trying to tell each other?

Dolphins call each other by name—with whistle signatures.

In southern Africa, people catch, squish, dry, and eat **giant caterpillars** called mopane worms.

Nom, nom. Which bugs are you serving for dinner?

Start the clock and find the 10 differences between these two batty scenes.

Professional basketball games **have been delayed by bats** that **flew around the court.**

Bonus activity!
Ask for permission to go online so you can check out Bracken Cave, in Texas, U.S.A, the home of the world's largest bat colony. There's lots of cool information and pictures—even a webcam! Go to *batcon.org/our-work/regions/usa-canada/protect-mega-populations/bracken-cave.*

Birds don't sweat.

These birds are keeping their cool on a hot summer day. What do you think they are saying?

Kite fighting
is a national sport
in Thailand.

What are they fighting about? Just kidding! Find the kite that is different from the others in each row.

Just in case you don't speak French, our fill-in-the-blanks game is in English—and it's your turn. Fill in the empty spaces to create words about nature.

F
DO PIN A IN
O W
W L
R R L
I VE
E N
E T TIDES
H U
N NA E EP ILE
T E ON
O EAN
LA DI I
D CLA AL
ST E
L

141

More than 7,000 languages are spoken worldwide.

C'est beaucoup de langues! Find wonderful ways to say "hello" around the globe. Words may be found horizontally, vertically, or diagonally, and forward or backward.

```
            B H U J M
            A K U M U S T A
          M O L Z O Z D U P
          I A W I H C I N N O K
        M Z C J A M A R H A B A K
      E O Y E S A H G N O E Y N N A
      Y L H D C B S O H B K S I O L O
      O A I C O A X I J M U A R L O
      S H H G Z C N I B A M L A H H
        S E S V E I K I J U U B A Z
        Z D R A V S T V U Y T A S
          S A L H U C T H R I H
          V E T S A M A N E
          O A H C N I X
            H A L L O
```

ahoj (Czech Republic)	**hej** (Sweden & Denmark)	**salut** (France)
annyeonghaseyo (North & South Korea)	**hola** (Mexico)	**shalom** (Israel)
bog (Croatia)	**hujambo** (Kenya)	**sveiki** (Lithuania)
ciao (Italy)	**konnichiwa** (Japan)	**üdzözlöm** (Hungary)
cześć (Portugal)	**kumusta** (Philippines)	**xin chào** (Vietnam)
habari (Swahili)	**marhaba** (Egypt)	**yahsahs** (Greece)
hallo (Germany & Netherlands)	**namaste** (India)	**zdravstvuyta** (Russia)

Grab a pencil and tell us about a law or resolution you would like to have enacted in your city or town and who or what it would help!

King Rama IV of Siam (Thailand) offered to send **elephants** to the U.S. as a gift; President **Abraham Lincoln** turned him down.

That was probably a wise decision——elephants are mostly at home in grasslands, savannas, and forests. What was a tough decision you made that you are proud of? Write it down here.

A GERMAN ROBOT learned how to MAKE PANCAKES.

Robots are running this household! Draw your own futuristic house, complete with helper robots. What are they doing?

Teams of SOCCER-PLAYING ROBOTS compete every year at the ROBOCUP.

145

In 12TH-CENTURY CHINA, people wore SUNGLASSES with LENSES made from QUARTZ, a type of crystal.

It's a bright and sunny day! Design some sunglasses for these cool kids.

The 16th-century Italian painter **Giuseppe Arcimboldo** **painted** fruits and **vegetables** to look like **human faces.**

Plant some silly expressions on these fruits and veggies.

Most of Earth's species are still undiscovered.

Imagine you are on an underwater expedition: What's the strangest species you will discover? Draw it and document it for science.

Hippos make their own sunscreen by oozing a thick red substance called "blood sweat."

That's gross—but pretty handy! These happy hippos are gathering at the watering hole. Color in their savanna scene.

In the sixth century, silkworm eggs were smuggled out of China so the Roman Empire could make its own silk.

These silkworm eggs could use a little sprucing up! Decorate them in your favorite patterns and colors.

Engineers have created a
BANDAGE
that **LIGHTS UP,**
TAKES YOUR TEMPERATURE,
and GIVES YOU MEDICINE.

A cut always seems to hurt less when your bandage is fun! **Decorate these bandages.**

The island of **MAURITIUS** in the Indian Ocean has **MULTICOLORED SAND DUNES.**

Wish you were there?! Create some postcards from these spots or other wacky places you've been to or have read about.

Greetings from ...

Wish You Were Here!

A rock in
JOSHUA TREE NATIONAL PARK
in California, U.S.A.,
resembles a giant
HUMAN SKULL.

START

You can ride the world's
TALLEST SLIDE—
four stories!—at an airport in Singapore.

Wheee! Do you have the stomach for that kind of ride? Slip and slide down this steep waterslide into the pool below.

Architects attached a
GLASS SLIDE
to the outside of a **72-story building** in Los Angeles, California, U.S.A.

FINISH

World Cup mascots have included a stick figure, a smiling orange, a sombrero-wearing chili pepper, and a trio of aliens.

T-E-A-M! You're the owner of a team, and it's time to create a mascot. **Tell us about** *your idea and draw it here.*

155

The world's largest lunch box museum, in Georgia, U.S.A., has more than 2,000 lunch boxes and thermoses.

Is it lunchtime yet? Design your own lunch box and one for a friend.

The first TV toy commercial advertised Mr. Potato Head.

You've created a brand-new toy, and you want everyone to enjoy it. Create a cool advertisement showing your awesome new invention!

31

EUROPA

Frankenstein

Frankenstein
has appeared on a
postage stamp
twice.

Do you think he scared the mail
carriers? Design your
own sets of stamps.
They don't have to be scary!

Some spiders spin webs longer than two city buses.

That's a sticky situation! Decide what—or who!—got caught in this wide web.

ANSWERS

Page 13

*These two answers can be switched.

Page 14

Page 19

Page 22

ANSWERS

Page 34

A man once **LICKED** every **cathedral** in England.

You should never, ever lick a cathedral—or any building! But it's safe to get close to this word search, where you'll find art and architecture terms throughout. Words may be found horizontally, vertically, or diagonally, and forward or backward.

arch	cornice	joinery	spire
balcony	dome	mosaic	tower
bay	eaves	pier	turret
boss	facade	pillar	veranda
column	frieze	portal	window

SAINT PAUL'S CATHEDRAL

34

Page 37

Some jellyfish glow.

What enlightening information! See if you can spot the electrifying terms hidden in this word search. Words may be found horizontally, vertically, or diagonally, and forward or backward.

AMP
BATTERY
BIOLUMINESCENCE
CELL
CHARGE
CIRCUIT
CURRENT
DYNAMO
ELECTROCUTE
FIELD
LIGHTNING
POWER
SHOCK
SIGNAL
SOCKET
VOLTAGE
WATT

Lemons can power lightbulbs.

37

Pages 40–41

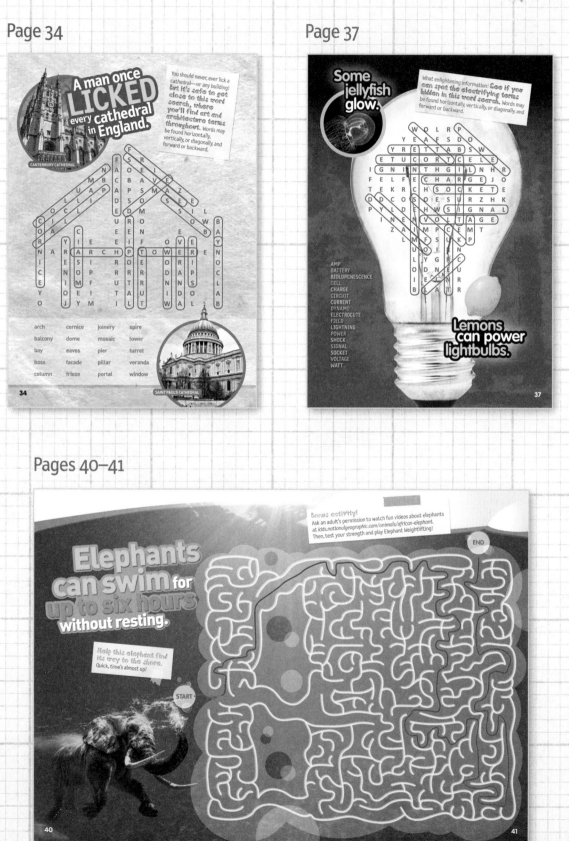

Elephants **can swim** for up to **six hours** without resting.

Help this elephant find its way to the shore. Quick, time's almost up!

START

Bonus activity!
Ask an adult's permission to watch fun videos about elephants at kids.nationalgeographic.com/animals/african-elephant. Then, test your strength and play Elephant Weightlifting!

END

40

41

ANSWERS

Page 42

There are approximately **three trillion TREES** on Earth.

And thousands of species! Find the names of 26 of them in this word search. Words may be found horizontally, vertically, or diagonally, and forward or backward.

```
E R D Y
M A G N O L I A
I T U I P O A K
R W I L L O W U W L D
O N G A M B H E O S Y E
E L P A M O C N R D
T U P E L O U R E
A M L O C U R H
Y R O K C A H
P O W D E R C U S T
O E O E M
W D E T L M
D E L A D
E R A D
```

ash   dogwood   holly   mulberry   spruce
elm   hickory   locust   oak   tulip
          magnolia   pine   tupelo
          maple   redwood   willow

42

Page 51

Snail **SLIME** can be used to **soften skin.**

Follow the trail of slime to the snail's hiding spot.

START

END 51

Page 55

BLOODHOUNDS can follow **a scent** that is **FOUR DAYS OLD.**

Help this hungry hound follow a scent to his bone!

START

END 55

Page 57

Find the 3 tiny garden gnomes in this yard—and 10 things that don't belong in a garden.

The world's **largest garden gnome** is **taller** than a giraffe.

57

ANSWERS

Page 69

There were more than **100** public holidays a year in ancient **Rome.**

Holidays

```
N A D A M A R E V O S S A P D
H T N A S A B E I L N Y E P I
A D A S O P A L T W O A T W E
S C H R I S T M A S X H A W S
D A E D E H T F O Y A D A E A
I N D E P E N D E N C E D A N
O B O N R M Y A K A U K V R R
Y A D G A L F S V W N Z E K A
H A K Y U P I N D A H A E G M
L O D O P K A L J Y T N N A A
P A L S V A D G M E Y R W E D
Y C H I N E S E N E W Y E A R
H A N U K K A H L O V I U M A
I G O N E W Y E A R S N D U P
```

That's cause for celebration! Find the holidays and traditions of past and present hidden in this word search. Words may be found horizontally, vertically, or diagonally, and forward or backward.

Abookyere · La Posada
Advent · Mardi Gras
Basanth · May Day
Chinese New Year · New Years
Christmas · Nyepi
Day of the Dead · O-Bon
Diwali · Onam
Easter · Passover
Flag Day · Ramadan
Hanukkah · Ridvan
Holi · Songkran
Independence Day · Thanksgiving
Kwanzaa

Now draw your favorite holiday memory.

69

Page 77

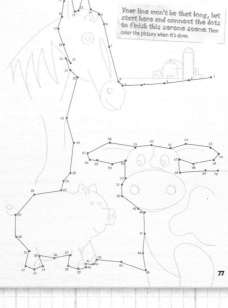

The average **pencil** has enough graphite to **draw a line** that's **35 miles** long. (56.3 km)

Your line won't be that long, but start here and connect the dots to finish this serene scene. Then color the picture when it's done.

77

Page 81

This Peep is lost! Help it find its way back to the candy store.

PEEPS had **WINGS** when they were first made.

START

END

candy-rama

There are enough **MARSHMALLOW PEEPS** made every year to **CIRCLE THE GLOBE TWICE.**

81

Page 84

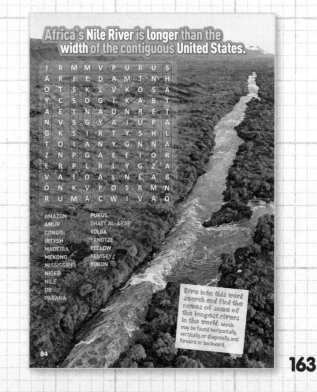

Africa's **Nile River** is **longer** than the width of the contiguous **United States.**

```
I R M M V P U R U S
A R I E D A M T N H
O T S K L V K O S A
Y C S O G I K A B T
A E I N A U N R E T
N V S G Y A I U P A
G K S I R T Y S H L
T O I A N Y G N N A
Z N P G A E E I O R
E R P L R L Y G Z A
V A I O A L N E A B
O N K V P O S R M N
R U M A C W I V A O
```

AMAZON · PURUS
AMUR · SHATT AL-ARAB
CONGO · VOLGA
IRTYSH · YANGTZE
MADEIRA · YELLOW
MEKONG · YENISEY
MISSISSIPPI · YUKON
NIGER
NILE
OB
PARANA

Dive into this word search and find the names of some of the longest rivers in the world. Words may be found horizontally, vertically, or diagonally, and forward or backward.

84

163

ANSWERS

Page 90

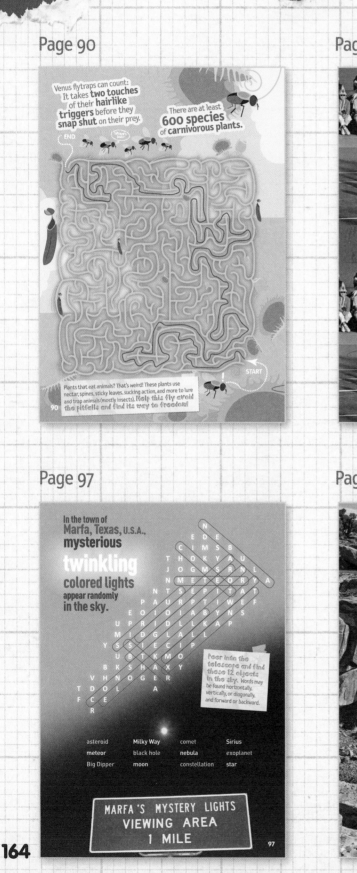

Venus flytraps can count: It takes **two touches** of their **hairlike triggers** before they **snap shut** on their prey.

There are at least **600 species** of **carnivorous plants.**

END

START

Plants that eat animals? That's weird! These plants use nectar, spines, sticky leaves, sucking action, and more to lure and trap animals (mostly insects). **Help this fly avoid the pitfalls and find its way to freedom!**

90

Page 91

Find the seven differences between these two photographs of a tennis match.
Hint: The tennis balls are yellow!

Tennis balls used to be **black or white.** They were **changed to yellow** when it was discovered that **TV viewers** could **see them better.**

91

Page 97

In the town of **Marfa, Texas, U.S.A.,** **mysterious**

twinkling

colored lights appear randomly in the sky.

Peer into the telescope and find these 12 objects in the sky. Words may be found horizontally, vertically, or diagonally, and forward or backward.

asteroid | Milky Way | comet | Sirius
meteor | black hole | nebula | exoplanet
Big Dipper | moon | constellation | star

MARFA'S MYSTERY LIGHTS
VIEWING AREA
1 MILE

97

Page 105

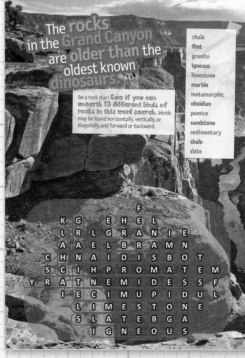

The **rocks** in the **Grand Canyon** are **older than the** oldest known **dinosaurs.**

chalk
flint
granite
igneous
limestone
marble
metamorphic
obsidian
pumice
sandstone
sedimentary
shale
slate

Be a rock star! See if you can unearth 13 different kinds of rocks in this word search. Words may be found horizontally, vertically, or diagonally, and forward or backward.

ANSWERS

Page 119

You're not supposed to play with your food! But you can unscramble the names of the ones listed here.

IBCORLOC	BROCCOLI
AANNBA	BANANA
HPTESGITA	SPAGHETTI
TETLECU	LETTUCE
OCABN	BACON
CZUHICNI	ZUCCHINI

AEP	PEA
OATTOP	POTATO
NCHEKIC	CHICKEN
DARBE	BREAD
YTUGOR	YOGURT
EIC RCAME	ICE CREAM
PEPLA	APPLE
HIFS	FISH
CEIR	RICE

In a Scottish Haggis-Hurling Competition, people stand on top of barrels and **throw** the **pudding** up to **217 feet.**

At a summer festival in **Barnesville, Minnesota, U.S.A.,** wrestlers **compete** in a **ring filled** with **mashed potatoes.**

119

Page 121

Every 13 or 17 years, **millions of noisy cicadas** emerge from **underground.**

END

A male African cicada can make a **sound** as **loud** as a **power mower.**

These cicadas need to tunnel out to make it aboveground! Help them find their way to the top.

START

121

Page 123

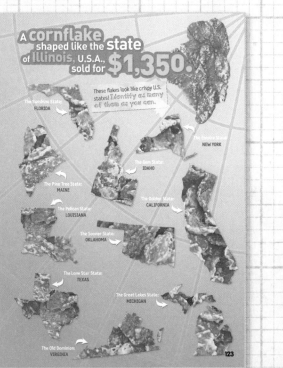

A **cornflake** shaped like the **state** of **Illinois**, U.S.A., sold for **$1,350.**

These flakes look like crispy U.S. states! Identify as many of them as you can.

The Sunshine State: FLORIDA

NEW YORK

The Gem State: IDAHO

The Pine Tree State: MAINE

The Golden State: CALIFORNIA

The Pelican State: LOUISIANA

The Sooner State: OKLAHOMA

The Lone Star State: TEXAS

The Great Lakes State: MICHIGAN

The Old Dominion: VIRGINIA

123

Page 132

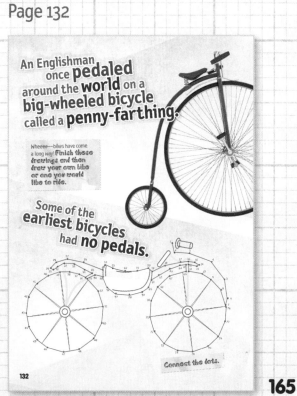

An Englishman once **pedaled** around the **world** on a **big-wheeled bicycle** called a **penny-farthing.**

Wheeee—bikes have come a long way! Finish these drawings and then draw your own bike or one you would like to ride.

Some of the **earliest bicycles** had **no pedals.**

Connect the dots.

132

165

ANSWERS

Page 135

Page 137

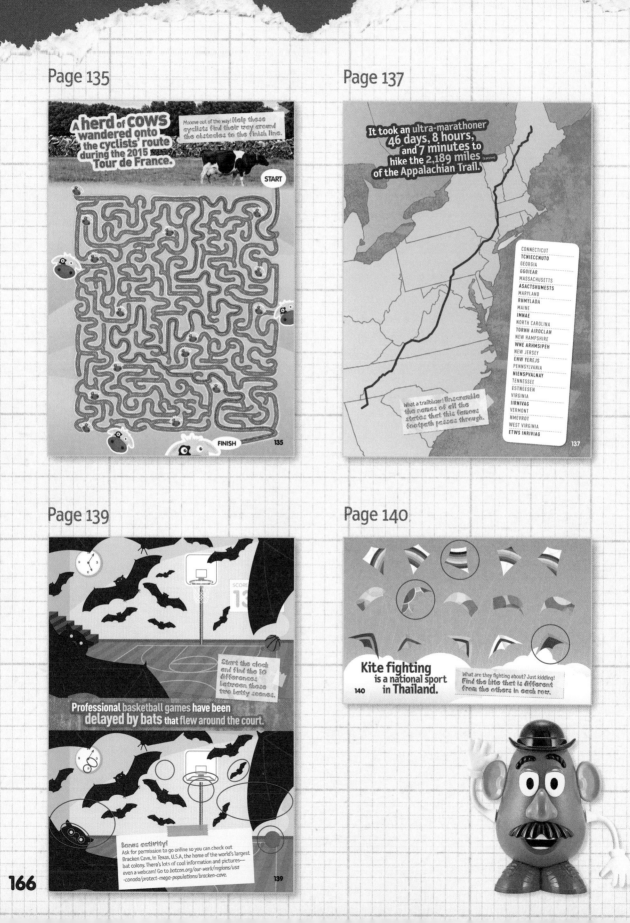

Page 139

Page 140

ANSWERS

Page 141

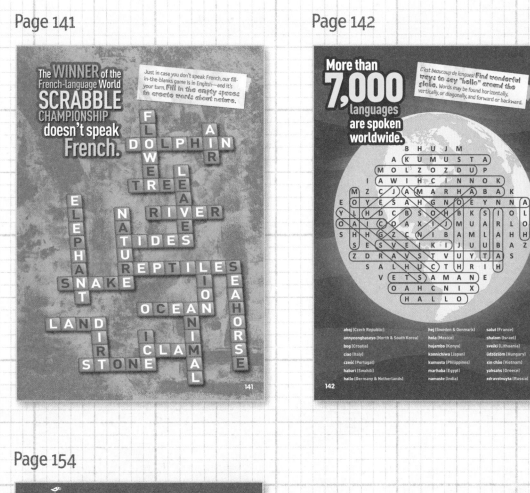

The **WINNER** of the French-language World **SCRABBLE** CHAMPIONSHIP **doesn't speak French.**

Just in case you don't speak French, our fill-in-the-blanks game is in English—and it's your turn. **Fill in the empty spaces to create words about nature.**

(Crossword solution:) DOLPHIN, AIR, FLOWER, LEAVES, TREE, NATURE, RIVER, ELEPHANT, TIDES, REPTILES, SNAKE, ACTION, OCEAN, SEAHORSE, LAND, DIRT, ANIMAL, CLAM, STONE

141

Page 142

More than 7,000 languages are spoken worldwide.

C'est beaucoup de langues! **Find wonderful ways to say "hello" around the globe.** Words may be found horizontally, vertically, or diagonally, and forward or backward.

(Word search grid with hidden words)

ahoj (Czech Republic)
annyeonghaseyo (North & South Korea)
bog (Croatia)
ciao (Italy)
cześć (Portugal)
habari (Swahili)
hallo (Germany & Netherlands)
hej (Sweden & Denmark)
hola (Mexico)
hujambo (Kenya)
konnichiwa (Japan)
kumusta (Philippines)
marhaba (Egypt)
namaste (India)
salut (France)
shalom (Israel)
sveiki (Lithuania)
üdvözlöm (Hungary)
xin chào (Vietnam)
yahsahs (Greece)
zdravstvuyta (Russia)

142

Page 154

You can ride the world's **TALLEST SLIDE**— four stories!—at an airport in Singapore.

Wheee! Do you have the stomach for that kind of ride? **Flip and slide down this steep waterslide into the pool below.**

Architects attached a **GLASS SLIDE** to the outside of a **72-story building** in Los Angeles, California, U.S.A.

START / FINISH

CREDITS

Word searches and crosswords created by Julie K. Cohen

Illustrations by Kevin McFadin unless otherwise noted

FRONT COVER: (LE), stockphoto mania/Shutterstock; (RT), Vitaly Titov/Shutterstock; (pencil), Ruslan Ivantsov/Shutterstock; Butterfly Hunter/Shutterstock; (panda), Eric Isselee/Shutterstock; (owl), QiuJu Song/Shutterstock; **SPINE:** (hamster), Subbotina Anna/Shutterstock; (pencil), Ruslan Ivantsov/Shutterstock; **BACK COVER:** (hot air balloon), Thanapun/Shutterstock; (lollipop), rangizzz/Shutterstock; (armadillo), Robert Eastman/Shutterstock; (dog), Rebecca Hale/National Geographic Creative; (pig), Tsekhmister/Dreamstime

INTERIOR: (LE), stockphoto mania/Shutterstock; (RT), Vitaly Titov/Shutterstock; 3 (UP RT), Nicescene/Shutterstock; 3 (LO LE), Linda Bucklin/Shutterstock; 3 (LO RT), Tui De Roy/Minden Pictures; 4 (UP), Kucher Serhii/Shutterstock; 4 (CTR), Baris Simsek/Getty Images; 4 (LO LE), zts/Dreamstime; 5 (LO), Richard Waters/Shutterstock; 5 (LO RT), Rebecca Hale/National Geographic Creative; 6 (UP), Geoff Moon/Minden Pictures; 7 (UP), ullstein bild/Getty Images; 8 (LO), Monticello/Dreamstime; 8 (LO LE), Monticello/Dreamstime; 8-9 (LO LE), limpido/Dreamstime; 8-9 (throughout), photka/Shutterstock; 9 (UP RT), O.Bellini/Shutterstock; 10 (CTR), Sculpies/Dreamstime; 11, Wojciech Skora/Shutterstock; 13 (UP), Cynthia Kidwell/Shutterstock; 13 (UP LE), Ian Maton/Shutterstock; 13 (CTR RT), Svetlana Foote/Dreamstime; 13 (CTR RT), Tom Reichner/Shutterstock; 13 (LO LE), Xbrchx/Dreamstime; 13 (LO CTR), Moose Henderson/Dreamstime; 13 (LO RT), Paul Reeves/Dreamstime; 14 (UP LE), Andrea Izzotti/Shutterstock; 14 (CTR), robertharding/Alamy Stock Photo; 14 (CTR), Marevision/Getty Images; 14 (CTR), Marjan Visser/Dreamstime; 14 (CTR), Rodger Klein/Getty Images; 14 (CTR), Hal Beral/Getty Images; 14 (CTR), Richcarey/Getty Images; 14 (LE), RomanMr/Shutterstock; 14 (CTR RT), WhitcombeRD/Getty Images; 14 (CTR RT), Rich Carey/Shutterstock; 14 (LO LE), Hal Beral/Getty Images; 15 (UP RT), Timekeeperwp/Dreamstime; 15 (LO LE), stockphoto mania/Shutterstock; 17 (UP RT), Bruce Campbell; 20 (UP RT), Alastair Wallace/Shutterstock; 21 (UP LE), Europics/Newscom; 21 (throughout), ShutterStock/Shutterstock; 23 (UP RT), Catmando/Shutterstock; 26 (LO RT), Stefano Buttafoco/Dreamstime; 27 (CTR), Pancaketom/Dreamstime; 28 (UP), Chris Hill/NG Creative; 28 (CTR LE), Chris Hill/NG Creative; 30 (CTR), Triff/Shutterstock; 30 (UP), Yury Dmitrienko/Shutterstock; 31 (UP LE), chrisdorney/Shutterstock; 32 (UP), Pixelrobot/Dreamstime; 32 (CTR), Anna Kucherova/Shutterstock; 33 (LO RT), Carrienelson1/Dreamstime; 34 (UP LE), Claudiodivizia/Dreamstime; 34 (LO RT), Marc Scott-Parkin/Shutterstock; 36 (UP LE), Splash News/Newscom; 37 (UP LE), Jurgen Freund/Minden Pictures; 37 (CTR), David Koscheck/Dreamstime; 37 (CTR RT), Danny Smythe/Dreamstime; 38 (UP RT), Richard Waters/Shutterstock; 38 (CTR), BlueOrange Studio/Shutterstock; 39 (LO), 2xSamara.com/Shutterstock; 40-41 (CTR), Willyam Bradberry/Shutterstock; 42 (UP), Nikolai Sorokin/Dreamstime; 42 (LO), Hero Images/Getty Images; 43 (UP RT), Dennis W Donohue/Shutterstock; 43 (LO LE), Pete Oxford/Minden Pictures; 44 (UP LE), DIDIER BOY DE LA TOUR; 47 (LO LE), Rudmer Zwerver/Dreamstime; 49 (LO), Tui De Roy/Minden Pictures; 50 (LO), Vitaly Titov/Shutterstock; 51 (UP), Emil Zhelyazkov/Dreamstime; 52 (LO), Photodisc; 53 (UP CTR), Veleknez/Dreamstime; 53 (CTR LE), Linda Bucklin/Shutterstock; 54 (UP LE), Jason Edwards/Getty Images; 54 (LO LE), Print Collector/Getty Images; 55 (UP), Rebecca Hale/National Geographic Creative; 57 (LO RT), Gunter Marx/Alamy; 58 (UP RT), Joel Sartore/National Geographic Creative; 59 (LO), Juniors Bildarchiv/Alamy Stock Photo; 60 (UP LE), Nicole Kucera/Getty Images; 62 (LE), B2AKF8/Alamy Stock Photo; 62-63 (CTR), Antikwar/Shutterstock; 64 (UP LE), Everett Historical/Shutterstock; 64 (LO), Chones/Shutterstock; 65 (UP LE), Mark Blinch/Reuters; 65 (LO RT), Culture Club/Getty Images; 66 (LO LE), Lonely Planet Images/Getty Images; 66 (UP RT), Hugh Chisholm; 68 (UP RT), Vispix.com/National Geographic Creative; 68 (CTR RT), RIEGER Bertrand/Getty Images; 70 (UP LE), Liz Rubert Pugh; 72 (UP LE), Charles Phoenix; 74 (CTR RT), Steve Heap/Shutterstock; 74 (CTR RT), Jagodka/Shutterstock; 74 (LO LE), Adogslifephoto/Dreamstime; 75 (LO), Javier Brosch/Shutterstock; 76 (UP LE), Foodio/Shutterstock; 76 (LO RT), PYT Burger & Bar; 77 (UP RT), Svitlana Zakharevich/Dreamstime; 80 (UP), Luke Farmer/Alamy Stock Photo; 81 (UP), Arinahabich08/Dreamstime; 81 (LO LE), Arinahabich08/Dreamstime; 82-83 (LO), Alain Lacroix/Dreamstime; 82 (LE), Christos Georghiou/Shutterstock; 83 (LO RT), 526751216/Getty Images; 84 (CTR), Gallo Images/Getty Images; 86-87 (LO), shipiolik/Getty Images; 86 (LO LE), Mario Tama/Getty Images; 87 (UP RT), AP Photo/Mike Brantley; 89 (UP RT), Anna Kucherova/Shutterstock; 91 (UP), Dana Gardner/Shutterstock; 91 (LO), Dana Gardner/Shutterstock; 91 (CTR), Pavlo Kucherov/Dreamstime; 92 (UP), Matthijs Kuijpers/Dreamstime; 96 (LO), National Aquarium of New Zealand; 96 (UP LE), Derek Lovley/Science Source; 97 (LO), RGB Ventures/Alamy Stock Photo; 98 (background), Idaho Fish & Game; 98 (UP LE), Idaho Fish & Game; 98 (UP RT), Idaho Fish & Game; 98 (LO), Pat Gaines/Getty Images; 99 (LE), luxora/Shutterstock; 99 (UP), Darren J. Bradley/Shutterstock; 99 (LO RT), aquapix/Shutterstock; 100 (UP), CaseyMartin/Shutterstock; 100 (LO), IMAGEMORE Co, Ltd./Getty Images; 101 (UP LE), SuperStock/Getty Images; 102 (UP RT), mjoo07/Getty Images; 103 (LO RT), Bernhard Richter/Shutterstock; 104 (LO LE), CB2/ZOB/Supplied by WENN/Newscom; 105 (CTR), sumikophoto/Shutterstock; 106 (UP), Sun Sentinel/Getty Images; 108 (RT), Andrey Pavlov/Dreamstime; 110 (UP), Karen Carr; 111 (UP LE), jbmake/Shutterstock; 111 (LO RT), Matee Nuserm/Shutterstock; 112 (UP LE), ricochet64/Shutterstock; 113 (UP), Minszka/Shutterstock; 114 (UP LE), Tuul and Bruno Morandi/Getty Images; 116 (CTR), Sunberry Fitness & Bandaids for Bunnies Shelter; 119 (UP), AP Photo/Press Association; 119 (LO), Prisma Bildagentur/Alamy Stock Photo; 120 (CTR), Dudarev Mikhail/Shutterstock; 120 (UP LE), Manfred Ruckszio/Shutterstock; 120 (UP RT), photomaster/Shutterstock; 121 (UP), Brand X Pictures/Getty Images; 121 (LO), Dave Bredeson/Dreamstime; 121 (LO), Pichet Panyaud/Dreamstime; 122 (UP RT), Ashwood/Getty Images; 123 (UP RT), AP Photo/The Virginian-Pilot, John H. Sheally II; 123 (CTR), anon_tae/Shutterstock; 124 (UP LE), Judith Dzierzawa/Dreamstime; 125 (UP RT), FloridaStock/Shutterstock; 125 (LO), Phil Torres; 126 (UP RT), critterbiz/Shutterstock; 126 (LO LE), Mikael Males/Shutterstock; 127 (UP LE), Odelia Cohen/Dreamstime; 127 (LO RT), Jose Manuel Gelpi Diaz/Dreamstime; 128 (LO), Ppy2010ha/Dreamstime; 129 (CTR RT), Aksenova Natalya/Shutterstock; 129 (LE), Vasyl Helevachuk/Dreamstime; 129 (UP), Inna Astakhova/Shutterstock; 130 (LO), maxim ibragimov/Shutterstock; 131 (CTR), Aflo Co. Ltd./Alamy Stock Photo; 131 (UP RT), Aflo Co. Ltd./Alamy Stock Photo; 132 (CTR), Baris Simsek/Getty Images; 134 (LO LE), asawinimages/Shutterstock; 134 (LO RT), Jitchanamont/Shutterstock; 135 (UP), Lars Ronbog/Getty Images; 136 (LO), Gladkova Svetlana/Shutterstock; 138 (UP), Gumenyuk Dmitriy/Shutterstock; 138 (CTR LE), Ioana Grecu/Dreamstime; 138 (CTR RT), Ricardo Canino/Shutterstock; 138 (LO LE), Altaoosthuizen/Dreamstime; 143, jeep2499/Shutterstock; 146 (LO), Stefano Cavoretto/Shutterstock; 147 (UP), Imagno/Getty Images; 148 (CTR), Pete Atkinson/Getty Images; 151 (UP LE), Melanie Gonick/MIT; 152 (UP LE), Oleg Znamenskiy/Shutterstock; 153 (LO RT), Lunamarina/Dreamstime; 155 (UP LE), Bob Thomas/Getty Images; 155 (LO RT), Choo Youn Kong/Getty Images; 156 (CTR), Gregory Wolkins; 157 (UP RT), Nicescene/Shutterstock; 158 (UP LE), HiPix/Alamy Stock Photo; 159 (LO), David Hilcher/Shutterstock; 162 (CTR), jbmake/Shutterstock; 166 (LO RT), Nicescene/Shutterstock; 167 (LO RT), Vitaly Titov/Shutterstock

STICKER PAGE 1: (clownfish), Bluehand/Dreamstime; (dog), Shevs/Dreamstime; (dragonfly), Subbotina/Dreamstime; (pink gem), 2ndpic/Dreamstime; (worm), Valentina Razumova/Dreamstime; (snail), zts/Dreamstime; (rabbit), iStockphoto; (Popsicle), Michael Gray/Dreamstime; (nose and glasses), RTimages/Shutterstock; (armadillo), Robert Eastman/Shutterstock; (soccer ball), irin-k/Shutterstock; (hot air balloon), Thanapun/Shutterstock; (shark), cbpix/Shutterstock; (lollipop), rangizzz/Shutterstock; (disco ball), Misunseo/

Shutterstock; (kangaroo), Anan Kaewkhammul/Shutterstock; (rocket), andrea crisante/Shutterstock; (butterfly), Butterfly Hunter/Shutterstock; (suitcase), Africa Studio/Shutterstock; (waffle), marla dawn studio/Shutterstock; (playing card), Christos Georghiou/Shutterstock; (rose), Anna Kucherova/Shutterstock; (penny-farthing), Baris Simsek/Getty Images; (astronaut), stockphoto mania/Shutterstock; **STICKER PAGE 2:** (baseball and mitt), Svetlana Larina/Dreamstime; (clownfish), Bluehand/Dreamstime; (pig), Tsekhmister/Dreamstime; (man in armor), iStockphoto; (origami), Photka/Dreamstime; (grapes), Valentyn Volkov/Shutterstock; (giraffe), Isselee/Dreamstime; (baby chimp), Eric Isselee/Shutterstock; (Earth), robert_s/Shutterstock; (raccoon), Sonsedska Yuliia/Shutterstock; (tropical flower), senlektomyum/Shutterstock; (sunflower), Yuliyan Velchev/Shutterstock; (lamb), Eric Isselee/Shutterstock; (Lego), galichstudio/Shutterstock; (pineapple), Jiri Miklo/Shutterstock; (watermelon slice), Nipaporn Panyacharoen/Shutterstock; (popcorn), Stephen Mcsweeny/Dreamstime; (wheel), Lajo_2/Shutterstock; (sea star), Darren J. Bradley/Dreamstime; **STICKER PAGE 3:** (teddy bear), Ovydyborets/Dreamstime; (penguins), Kotomiti_okuma/Dreamstime; (ladybug), Alexstar/Dreamstime; (lion), Isselee/Dreamstime; (magic lamp), Fernando Gregory/Dreamstime; (origami), Photka/Dreamstime; (rainbow lorikeet), Eric Isselee/Shutterstock; (balloons), artjazz/Shutterstock; (birthday hat), Stacy Barnett/Shutterstock; (donut), Demkat/Shutterstock; (key), azurei/Shutterstock; (clown shoes), Elena Schweitzer/Shutterstock; (strawberry), Valentina Razumova/Shutterstock; (whoopee cushion), Mega Pixel/Shutterstock; (rubber chicken), Lightzoom/Dreamstime; (tree frog), Dirk Ercken/Dreamstime; (rabbit in hat), Ljupco/Dreamstime; (lightbulb), udra/Shutterstock; **STICKER PAGE 4:** (horse), Kseniya Abramova/Dreamstime; (yellow car), Len Green/Dreamstime; (duckling), Levente Gyori/Dreamstime; (gumballs), Kelpfish/Dreamstime; (cheetah), Ana Vasileva/Dreamstime; (treasure chest), Aprilphoto/Shutterstock; (cookie), Sergio33/Shutterstock; (sitting cat), Africa Studio/Shutterstock; (egg), Valentina Razumova/Shutterstock; (piñata), Mega Pixel/Shutterstock; (smiling cat), Utekhina Anna/Shutterstock; (chicken), Valentina_S/Shutterstock; (roller skates), igorstevanovic/Shutterstock; (lemon), Nerss/Dreamstime; (pigeon), Vitaly Titov/Shutterstock; (moth), jbmake/Shutterstock; (pineapple), Jiri Miklo/Shutterstock

Since 1888, the National Geographic Society has funded more than 12,000 research, exploration, and preservation projects around the world. The Society receives funds from National Geographic Partners, LLC, funded in part by your purchase. A portion of the proceeds from this book supports this vital work. To learn more, visit natgeo.com/info.

NATIONAL GEOGRAPHIC and Yellow Border Design are trademarks of the National Geographic Society, used under license.

For more information, visit nationalgeographic.com, call 1-800-647-5463, or write to the following address:

National Geographic Partners
1145 17th Street N.W.
Washington, D.C. 20036-4688 U.S.A.

Visit us online at nationalgeographic.com/books

For librarians and teachers: ngchildrensbooks.org

More for kids from National Geographic: kids.nationalgeographic.com

For information about special discounts for bulk purchases, please contact National Geographic Books Special Sales: specialsales@natgeo.com

For rights or permissions inquiries, please contact National Geographic Books Subsidiary Rights: bookrights@natgeo.com

Art directed by Julide Dengel

Designed by Fan Works Design, LLC

Trade paperback ISBN: 978-1-4263-2788-9

Printed in China
17/PPS/1

The publisher would like to thank everyone who made this book possible, including Kate Hale, senior editor; Jen Agresta, project editor; Christina Ascani, associate photo editor; Avery Hurt, researcher; Alix Inchausti, production editor; and Anne LeongSon and Gustavo Tello, design production assistants.